Leo the Magnificat

Leo the Magnificat

ANN M. MARTIN

ILLUSTRATED BY EMILY ARNOLD McCULLY

SCHOLASTIC PRESS / NEW YORK

This book is for all the people who remember the real Leo, and of course it is for Leo the Magnificat himself. But most especially this book is for Laura.
— A. M. M.

For Lynn and Inky and in memory of Pookie
— E. A. M.

Thanks to those friends of Leo's who generously took the time to share their memories of him with me — my aunt and uncle, Adele and Paul Vinsel; the Right Reverend Allen Bartlett, Jr; the Very Reverend Geralyn Wolf; and Kay Sheilds Wilkinson. Thanks also to Laura Godwin, Jean Feiwel, and Bethany Buck, whose guidance was of inestimable value.

Library of Congress Cataloging-in-Publication Data
Martin, Ann M., 1955-
Leo the Magnificat / by Ann M. Martin; illustrated by Emily Arnold McCully. p. cm.
Summary: A homeless cat wanders into a small church and warms the hearts of the people there.
ISBN 0-590-48498-2
[1. Cats — Fiction. 2. Church — Fiction.] I. McCully, Emily Arnold, ill. II. Title. PZ7.M3567585Am 1996
[E] — dc20   95-33640
CIP   AC
12 11 10 9 8 7 6 5 4 3 2 1   6 7 8 9/9 0 1/0
Printed in the United States of America   36
First printing, October 1996
The text type was set in 15 pt. Dante.
The illustrations were created using watercolors and gouache.

ON A SUNDAY in November, a cat wandered into the garden of a church.

Mrs. Moody, the church secretary, found him there. He was sitting by the fountain.

"Hello. Where did you come from?" asked Mrs. Moody. She moved closer to the cat. The cat moved closer to Mrs. Moody. "Who do you belong to? You must belong to somebody. You're wearing a flea collar. And you look well fed."

"He's not well fed, he's fat!" exclaimed Allie.

"Extra fat," said Whitney.

The Sunday schoolers had followed Mrs. Moody into the garden. They gathered around the cat. The cat closed his eyes and purred.

"I think he's a she," said Kendall. "And she's going to have babies. That's why she's so fat."

"She needs a good name," said Allie.

The children named her Cleopatra.

No one ever found out where the cat had come from. Mrs. Moody placed an ad in the local newspaper. Nobody answered it. Reverend Neil said the cat could stay. But Mrs. Moody worried that Cleopatra was a wanderer.

Mrs. Moody took Cleopatra to the vet. The vet told her Cleo was a boy. But he did not know how old he was. "Goodness, he's fat," he added. "He'll need to go on a diet."

The children changed Cleo's name to Leo. Leo the Magnificat.

"Magnificat, from the Bible," said Allie. "Another good name. A good name for a church cat."

Leo the Magnificat made the church his home.

He attended meetings.

He went to choir practice.

He learned to let Mrs. Moody know when he wanted to come inside.
He was a guest at the covered-dish dinners.

Every Sunday, he went to the church service. If he was in a good
mood, he sang along with the choir.

His favorite bed was the sheep costume for the Christmas pageant. It was kept in a dark closet. Leo chose it himself.

Everybody loved Leo. Even people who didn't like cats liked Leo. Reverend Neil gave him a clerical collar to wear on special church occasions. He called Leo "the Bishop."

The children gave him toys. They brought him a basket to sleep in. (Leo preferred the sheep costume, but sometimes he slept in the basket anyway.)

Mrs. Moody let Leo come and go, since he seemed to have plenty of errands to run. She worried that he would wander off, but he always returned to the church in time for meals.

Leo belonged to nobody, and he belonged to everybody.

Leo made friends everywhere, but especially at the church. One of his friends was Mr. Tate. Mr. Tate did not have a family. And he hated to cook. But he loved to eat. (So did Leo.)

Mr. Tate attended every one of the covered-dish dinners. He always fixed one plate of food for Leo and one plate of food for himself.

Another of Leo's friends was Miss Hadley. Miss Hadley did not have a family either. However, she loved to cook. And to eat. She carried a container of tuna fish in her purse for Leo. (Leo's diet was not going well.)

Leo encouraged Miss Hadley and Mr. Tate to sit together in church.

Before long, they got married.
Leo went to the wedding.

Every day, Leo met some of his best friends in his favorite spot, the garden. Mose and Agatha and Walter lived on the streets. They had no homes, but they felt at home at the church. Leo seemed to understand.

Sometimes they came to church for the covered-dish dinners. Sometimes they didn't. But no matter what, rain or shine, they visited with Leo at lunchtime. If they had any extra food, they shared it with him. After all, Leo had once been homeless, too.

The rest of Leo's best friends were every single one of the children who came to the church. Allie and Whitney and Kendall and their friends. They hugged him when they felt sad. They hugged him when they felt happy. They let him help out during the Christmas pageant.

Leo had a lot to do around the church.

One morning Mrs. Moody couldn't find Leo. He wasn't in the closet sleeping on the sheep costume. He wasn't in his basket. Most surprising, he did not go to the garden at noontime.

Mose knocked on the door to Mrs. Moody's office. "Where's the cat?" he asked. "I brought him baloney."

Now, Leo could smell baloney from miles away. "Oh, dear," said Mrs. Moody. Then she added, "I knew it. I knew Leo would not stay. That cat is a wanderer."

But Mose replied, "I don't think so. Something has happened. We better look for him."

So the search for Leo began.

Suppertime came. Leo had not turned up. "Oh, dear," said Mrs. Moody again. "He has never missed a meal. Now he has missed two."

Nighttime came. Leo's basket was empty. The sheep costume sat alone in the closet.

Mrs. Moody asked the members of the choir if they had seen Leo. Nobody had.

Reverend Neil scratched his head. "I wonder what we should do now," he said.

Mose and Agatha and Walter were in the garden. Mrs. Moody and
Reverend Neil joined them. They were standing there when a cab pulled
up outside.

The driver opened his window. "Evening," he said. "I got your cat here. Must have jumped in when I wasn't looking. He's been riding around with me all afternoon. I was about to take him to the pound when my last passenger recognized him. So I brought him back."

The driver opened the back door of his cab. Leo hopped out. "Mrrow," he said to Mrs. Moody. Then he trotted inside.

Leo never disappeared again. And he never missed another meal.

Time passed. Leo had lived at the church for twelve years. He was growing old. Reverend Neil had moved away. Reverend Wilson had taken his place. Mrs. Moody was still the secretary, but she was growing old, too. So were Mr. Tate and Mrs. Tate and Mose and Agatha and Walter. The Sunday schoolers were not children anymore. They had grown up. Allie was married and had a baby of her own. A new group of children went to Sunday school and performed in the Christmas pageant.

Leo spent more and more time sleeping on the sheep costume. Some days he did not feel well. Finally Mrs. Moody and Reverend Wilson took him to the vet.

One Sunday, Reverend Wilson stood before the people at the church. "Leo is very sick," she told them. "He's old and he's in pain. And the vet cannot make him feel better. So he is going to give Leo a shot that will help him die peacefully. Then Leo won't be in pain any longer."

Reverend Wilson looked at the empty spot in the pew where Leo usually sat. "Leo's funeral will be held on Wednesday," she told the people.

That afternoon, Leo rested in his old basket. He let everyone file past
to pat him and kiss him.

Three days later, Leo the Magnificat was buried by the fountain in the garden. Thirty people were there. Reverend Neil traveled one hundred miles to come to Leo's funeral.

Everyone talked about Leo and remembered the things they liked about him.

"He was only a cat," said Allie, "but he was my best friend."

"He helped us find each other," said Mr. and Mrs. Tate.

"He snitched my food," said Mose. "That cat had spirit."

"I could depend on him," said Agatha. "He was no ordinary cat."

"He chose us," said Mrs. Moody. "He chose us to be his family."

The people bowed their heads.

Reverend Wilson had made a wooden marker, and she set it on Leo's grave. "Good-bye, Leo," she said.

The True Story of Leo the Magnificat

Once upon a time, there really was a cat named Leo the Magnificat. He lived at Christ Church Episcopal Cathedral in Louisville, Kentucky, and this book is based on Leo's life there. Some of the incidents in the story are made up and some have been changed; all of the characters are made up. But Leo was quite real and every bit as beloved to the people who knew him as he was to the characters in the story.

The real Leo was a Siamese cat. He turned up at the church one day and simply stayed. No one knew where he had come from. He lived there for twelve years, had many adventures, and made lots of friends. When he died, a funeral was held for him, and he was buried in the garden of the church. A marker was placed there in his memory. No one who met Leo will ever forget him.

Photo: Olan Mills